HELP WANTED

$250,000 YEAR
SPOILT ROTTEN

EXTREME HORROR

From the dark mind of
Sea Caummisar

Help Wanted: Spoilt Rotten

From the dark mind of
Sea Caummisar

Copyright © 2022 by Sea Caummisar

All rights reserved. No portion of this book may be reproduced in any form without permission from the publisher, except as permitted by U.S. copyright law. For permissions contact sharoncheatham81@gmail.com

This is entirely a work of fiction, pulled out of my own imagination. All characters and events are not real (fictitious). If there are any similarities to real persons, living or dead, it is purely coincidental.

This story is pure fiction. It is not to discourage anyone from responding to help wanted signs. However, (especially in fiction) if something sounds too good to be true, then it is probably false.

Help Wanted: Spoilt Rotten	2
Book Description	6
Introduction	8
The Signs	9
Methods	13
The Invitation	17
The Meet	21
Finalized Plans	25
The Job	28
Beginning	29
Welcome	33
Wake	38
And Wax	42
Teaching the Job	48
The Punishment Room	52
Niceties	57
New Duties	62
Maid Duties	66
Change of Employee	69
On the Home Front	70
Welcomed	72
Friendships?	76

Dinner	80
Animosity	84
A Show	88
Stillness	93
Fighting Chances	97
Testing Limits	100
Actualities	105
Cold, Bitter, Truths	106
More of Omer's Suffering	109
Axel's Suffering	114
Axie-Poo, The Pet	117
Golfing with Axie-Poo	120
Bath Time w/ Axie-Poo	122
Playtime w/ Axie-Poo	125
Future Plans (During Another Show)	129
A note from my dark mind	131

Book Description

Help Wanted: $250,000 USD for one year of work.
Full time: 8760 hours. 24 hours a day/ 7 days a week/ 365 days
Location: Isolated and private
Duties: Light cooking/ cleaning/ etc… Anything and everything
Title: Assistant (assisting me with all my needs and wants)
Requirements: The desire to make money. Someone ambitious with a strong work ethic.

The story of a wealthy woman hiring an assistant to fulfill all of her needs and wants.
A lawyer who hires a private investigator to put an end to her evil deeds.

Characters
Terrence - lawyer
Axel - private investigator
Lilith - wealthy heiress
Leo - Lilith's security guard
Omer- new employee

Introduction

The Signs

"This is your part of the job!" Lilith screamed into the phone. "Why are you bugging me again? What am I paying you for?"

Five thousand miles away, her lawyer sat behind his desk and loosened his neck tie. The glass walls of his office seemed inappropriate in times like now. If his co-workers (even though most of them were in his employ) saw anger on his face, they might form a negative opinion of him. Quickly, he shuffled his feet and rotated his chair so that his back was turned away from them.

Terrance gazed upon what most would call a beautiful view of the city. All he saw was pollution, grime, and garbage. If he looked hard enough, he would even see a tent camp of homeless people several blocks away. "I'm still here in New York City. Laws apply to me. My law license is at stake. I wrote the contract. I gave you my contacts and you can deal with them directly. They are all trusted by me. Mostly because they don't know much of anything and I keep them in the dark. It must be nice nestled in safety on your private island, but I live in civilization. I have to be careful. Each time gets worse. Especially after the last one…"

"Last year was a fluke, so don't go there. Can't you do this for me? One more time? You always handle these matters," Lilith spoke calm and peacefully. "Pretty please? I don't like the sound of Axel's voice. What kind of name is Axel, anyway?"

She raised her glass, clinking the ice cubes together, signaling her bodyguard that she was in need of more drink. Normally that wasn't his job, but he was the only other staff present.

Leo took the hint, grabbed her glass and tended to it behind the bar.

"I can't do it," Terrence sighed heavily in the phone. "I will still be your legal representative if the need arises. Write contracts and such, but that's it. I already told you, I trust him. Work with him."

"What if I offer you another million?"

"Offer Axel the million. He'll be thrilled. I'm sure."

"You're the only reason, T, that I do it this way. Legally. I could kidnap some poor soul and do it against their will."

"Sorry, darling," he replied, and almost pushed the button to end the call. "Don't put this on me. You like it my way better. Remember telling me that? You like it when they're willing. It's part of your mind game. You like paying them and get off on the control you have over them. You like the typical things that money shouldn't be able to buy."

After Lilith made a *humph* sound, the lawyer ended the call. It was a satisfying feeling. Now, with his eyes fully open, he surveyed the other skyscrapers, realizing he was fortunate that his building was among the tallest.

"Perspective," he noted aloud. "Keep things in perspective."

Turning back to face the glass walls that caged him, he pasted a large smile on his face. Determined to not fall into the stereotypical categories that the majority of society labeled lawyers, attorneys, and solicitors, Terrence took another step to absolving himself.

"Did you catch all that? Did you get it recorded?" he asked Axel.

Axel nodded and leaned forward to shut off the electronic equipment. "I did, but there's still no proof of a crime. This is a lot of work, and it only takes one criminal off the street. Even then, her private island isn't governed by a government like ours. Why hire me? I'm nobody but a private investigator. Don't get me wrong, I like catching bad people, but getting her arrested will be a stretch. If you weren't paying me so much, I wouldn't have even taken the case."

Still with the large grin, Terrence leaned back in his chair and propped his feet on his desk. "Wait. Watch and wait. It started simple with her. Each time she got more and more…" he paused trying to find the right word. "Chaotic. A young man lost his life last year. Not just a limb, or sometimes two, like the others. Lilith is an evil woman. If I could even damage her reputation. Make people see that she isn't the humanitarian they think she is. Paying you will be worth it. All I need is proof."

After a long silence of the two men staring at each other, Terrence sweetened the deal. "I'll pay you double if you convince her to commit a crime here, or even in a country with extradition laws."

"You heard her," Axel said as he gathered his equipment to leave. "She doesn't like the sound of my voice. Or my name. I doubt I'll be able to convince her to do anything."

Methods

"Yes, Ms. Tharn," Axel spoke into his computer, trying not to roll his eyes in front of the client. "I'm a bit overwhelmed by the responses. You wouldn't believe how many young males are willing to do whatever it takes to earn two hundred and fifty thousand dollars in a year. It would be easier if I could hire a team."

"Terrence never needed a team, I don't think," Lilith said, pointing her finger at her computer. "They'll weed out after the first contract. It explicitly says that it is for three hundred sixty-five days around the clock. Almost nine thousand straight hours of tending to my beck and call. The clause, where they will have no internet access or phone, is highlighted. No access to the outside world whatsoever. Are you competent or not?"

"Well, ma'am, this isn't so easy with you only allowing me to post the job listing in certain countries. You want them to speak English, but I can't post here in the USA, where I am. Why not? I don't even have the details of the job."

Aggravated, Lilith snapped her fingers, and Leo grabbed her empty glass off-screen. "I need Terrence back. He understands me. He handles the legal stuff and which countries are off limits."

"The part of wanting their family background, relationship status, all that. It's so specific and…"

"Yes, a loner would be best. They will cook, clean, and whatever else I require."

Feeling frustrated, Axel reminded himself of the money he was making. Normally, he dealt with spouses that had been cheated on, or relatives searching for long lost family members. Having to put up with a pompous socialite was a new experience. Occasionally, he worked for Terrence's law firm when they needed information on people.

Reluctantly, he agreed. "Okay, you're the boss."

With her freshened up drink, possibly dark liquor, Lilith smirked. "Repeat that. Your voice grates on my nerves, but what you said sparked joy inside of me."

"Huh?"

"I hate speaking through computer screens. I could fly you to me, and we could get acquainted properly. Discuss the details."

Going to her private island and learning exactly what she wanted could help him break the case, but something about how Terrence warned him of her filled him with fear. "I'm aware that you have internet access because I'm speaking to you through a computer right now. I have conditions if I come. Such as my telling people of where I'm going. Access to my phone."

"You're smarter than you look, in a rugged commoner way. Did Terrence tell you, or have you figured this out all by yourself?"

Once again, her condescending tone went through him like a heat wave. "You're paying too well for anything on the up and up. It doesn't take a genius to figure anything out that what you're hiring for can't be anything good."

Sipping from her glass, Lilith nodded. "I think I like you. Sure, I'll come to you. America, here I come. It's been a while since I've been there. It is my home, used to be, don't you know?"

"I'm well aware that you come from money. Hotels, apartments, any real estate really. An heiress, right?"

"Then you're aware why this is to be kept secret. I have a reputation to protect. That is, if I don't want my family to disown me. And I don't want that. I'll come to you. If Terrence trusts you, I suppose I should too. I've known him almost my whole life."

Axel watched as his screen turned black. It felt rather odd that she didn't ask for his address, or make any actual plans for them to meet. There was a tiny, nagging voice in the back of his mind telling him that he should be careful.

For a split second, he thought about calling Terrence and calling off the job. Could it be true that this hundred and twenty pound woman was a killer who enjoyed torturing people?

Then, he reminded himself that the kind of money that Terrence was offering him would set him up for the rest of his life.

The Invitation

Two days later, Axel found a white envelope slid under the door of his apartment. It listed an address and time to meet, but it wasn't signed. It did ask for him to bring the files of applicants, which was the only clue that it was regarding the job he had listed for Lilith.

The way a physical letter showed up randomly on his doorstep sent a chill down his spine. "She could call me. Haven't phones and email replaced snail mail?"

In his line of work, it was unusual that he had been the one being watched instead of the watcher. The meeting requested was for later that evening, and everything in his gut told him to call Terrence and call off the job. It felt wrong.

Before calling the man who employed him, he did a Google search of the address and found it was a posh restaurant on the other side of town. One that he could never afford since their meals averaged a thousand dollars a plate, not including drinks. Another hint that the envelope had been sent by Lilith.

Rather than worrying about meeting her, since the place was public and he was sure no harm would come to him, Axel wondered what kind of dress code he should abide by. In his line of work, it was necessary to blend in with the crowd and not stand out. Therefore, his wardrobe was full of casual clothing.

There was one suit hanging in his closet, black, and reserved for funerals and weddings. Short on time to go shopping, that suit would have to do.

The least he could do was shave his face, but not his soul patch. The tuft of hair below his lower lip was his pride and joy. A stylish expression he thought represented his usually carefree attitude. The stubble on his cheeks could be shaved off, which would highlight his perfect skin, making him appear younger than his age.

When he visited a wedding or funeral, he wore his shoulder length hair in a ponytail. As much as he loved his messy hairstyle, normally washed and allowed to air dry showing off the natural wave, he thought the ponytail would be best for an expensive restaurant.

His father had always told him to dress for the job he wanted, not the one he had. In this instance, he had a job he didn't want, but one he felt obliged to for financial reasons. The circumstance may have been backwards, but Axel decided that looking the role would be best.

In the shower, a small voice kept telling him that he should call someone and let them know his whereabouts that evening. Firstly, Lilith was a very private person, so he knew that he couldn't tell any of his friends or colleagues whom he was meeting. If word got out, it would blow his cover and Lilith could possibly fire him.

Secondly, how would he explain to anyone that knew him that he was dining at one of the most expensive restaurants in the world?

That left Terrence.

"She's here? In the states?" Terrence asked with a hint of excitement. "That's great news. Convince her to choose an 'employee'," making finger air quotes as he spoke the word, even though he was on the phone, "from here. I could get her then."

After telling Terrence where they were meeting, the other end of the phone went silent. "Are you there, Terrence?"

"Yeah. I'm here. Buckle up buddy. I've known her most of my adult life. She has more in store for you than dinner."

Axel was left holding his phone to his ear, hearing only blank air. "What's that mean? Terrence? Hello?"

There was no reply and the man had disconnected the call.

Thinking how strange this job had become, Axel wasn't sure if he was scared or excited.

The Meet

The man standing at the foyer of the restaurant was dressed simply in black slacks and a white button-down shirt.

"Hi. I have a reservation to meet-"

The man waved for Axel to follow him. "I know who you are. Right this way."

Being led through the restaurant and seeing the other diners made Axel feel overdressed. Many men were wearing polo shirts or sweaters. There was nobody as dressed up as him in a suit and tie. Feeling overdressed wasn't something he had considered.

Before reaching the back room, the man pulled back a velvet black curtain, and there were several empty tables. The only person was Lilith, seated center in the room.

She stood to greet her guest, revealing her expensive black jeans and a black tank top. "I see you're taking this job seriously?" she asked as he neared the table.

Suddenly even more aware of his attire, he sat down his leather briefcase and extended his arm for a handshake.

With both hands, Lilith placed her hands on both of his biceps. "So formal. Not necessary. I prefer to intertwine intimacy in my meetings." She gave a slight squeeze to both of his arms before sitting back down. "I used to bring Terrence here. He seemed to enjoy it."

His necktie had been practically choking him, and Axel's lungs felt deprived of air. To appear more casual, he loosened the knot and allowed the tie to hang loosely down his chest. "I brought the few candidates that I think you might like. Their pictures and their backgrounds-"

"Down to business, hmm? Let's enjoy our meal first. Then we'll discuss that. Tell me about yourself. How you know Terrence."

This was beginning to feel more like he was the one being interviewed, not offering her the applicants. "His law firm has used me on some cases. By trade, I'm a private investigator. If he needs dirt on someone, or to see how honest a witness is, he comes to me." After saying the words aloud, he wondered if he had told her too much.

Looking at her directly was like staring into the sun; blinded by beauty. The porcelain toned skin of her face was perfectly highlighted by a thin layer of blush on her cheeks. The pale pink painted onto her lips gave her an appearance of innocence. Her eyes, gray and large, flawless in symmetry, dazzled between her thick eyelashes.

Axel looked away, down at the cloth napkin he knew he should place in his lap.

"I gathered that much," Lilith noted with a sigh. "I want to know you. Specifics."

Taking his time and unfolding the napkin, Axel spent longer than he should on the task. Anything for his eyes to avoid meeting hers. "I offer each of my clients confidentiality. Even Terrence. A service I'm also extending to you."

"Same as Terrence told me. He says he trusts you," Lilith said coyly. "I know him well. Very well, if you catch my meaning. Very intimately. I've never known the man to trust anyone. Including me."

Hoping silently for anything to happen that would end the conversation, a waiter approached. "Would you like a wine list?"

Ignoring the man, Lilith reached across the table, and placed her hand on top of Axel's. "I wish you would have kept that rugged look for tonight. That stubble you had when we video chatted. Very sexy."

Not knowing how to respond, Axel's cheeks flushed, and looked up at the waiter. "I would love a cocktail."

"Bring him whatever he wants. I paid enough to rent out this back room, you should be able to read our minds."

The waiter must have been used to dealing with snobbish patrons, so he hung his head and apologized. "My sincerest apologies, madame. May I suggest to the gentleman a twenty-year Scotch? Or would he prefer something with more age?"

"Something older, definitely," Lilith answered for him.

Axel had a feeling she was referring to herself and not the drink. She may have had a decade on him in years, but she sure didn't look like it. He knew that he was in for a long night.

Finalized Plans

"I'm telling you, Terrence," Axel said, standing and staring at the incredible view above the bustling city. "Our meeting was strange, and I did all that I could do. I think it's impossible to go after her legally. You must have taught her well."

The sweaty lawyer was outdone with his private investigator. "How hard did you try?"

"I tried," Axel replied, finally sitting down on the couch across from the lawyer's large desk. "She didn't want an American employee. The second photo I showed her, she jumped right on it. She wanted him. She had me set up the pickup. Not only that, but she went the next day on her private plane to pick him up. It was out of my hands."

"What am I paying you for?"

"I guess nothing. I can't force her to do something illegal. Well, nothing illegal where the laws apply."

There were several underlings outside of his glass office walls, so Terrence was careful to not raise his voice. Maybe he cared too much what paralegals and secretaries thought of him, but it was something instilled in him. "You had sex with her?"

Calmly, Axel used a hand to rub the stubble of his face. "Is that a question? Or an accusation? Speaking from experience, huh?"

"Never mind that," Terrence sounded defeated. "What if you go to her island? Make some videos or something. Legalities or not, we could ruin her reputation. Do you know she recently donated millions to help with that hurricane relief down south? I can't stand the thought of her playing saint in the public eye, and villain in secret. You do know you put that boy in danger."

Axel shrugged. "That boy was an orphan. Running the streets for the past couple years. No blood family to mention. Willing to work for the money she offered. I quote, his words exactly, 'I'd do anything for that kind of money'. A quarter of a million dollars to what, be her sex slave for a year? That's a much better life than he had. Not a bad deal if you ask me. He saw the help wanted sign at some cafe. Saw a way to change his life. Anyway, she said that she doesn't do anything to them that they don't agree to."

Still trying to be civil and not fly off the handle, Terrence sighed, and took several deep breaths. "So she snowed you? Lied to you and you believed her?"

Feeling like he was overly repeating himself, Axel wanted an end to the conversation. "I tried. I guess I'll refund your money. What else could I have done?"

"No. Keep it. Let's put our heads together. I'll pay you more. As long as I get what I want."

All Axel could see were imaginary dollar signs floating in the air.

The Job

Beginning

The way the boy's lips curled upwards told Lilith all that she needed to know. Between the long plane ride and then the helicopter ride to her island, they had plenty of time to talk and get the small formalities out of the way. Omer looked so happy.

His olive-toned skin, darkened by days in the sun, highlighted his somewhat muscular arms. This wasn't the physique one earned by working out in a gym, but rather by manual labor, keeping him lean. Muscles toned but not well-defined. During their travels, he had mentioned working wherever he could find a job, including dump and construction sites carrying and lifting, for menial pay.

However, work wasn't consistent.

With Omer being young, claiming he was twenty but barely looked sixteen, what he lacked in experience, her security guard, Leo, had an advantage. If- no, when- push came to shove, Leo would have no difficulty forcing the younger man to comply to her wishes.

Hearing Omer's story of losing his parents and living on the streets bored Lilith, but she gave him the opportunity to tell all. A ploy to make him feel comfortable when he shouldn't.

His cellular phone had been a pre-pay, one that currently had no money nor time left on it, which definitely pleased Lilith. When she warned him that her island provided no communication with the outside world, Omer told her that it didn't matter. If that was part of his job, he would happily oblige.

Eventually, the boy fell asleep and Lilith watched him.

Leo offered, but she had been the one to wake Omer when the plane landed, with a welcoming look on her face. Leo was a hired hand, particularly for his ways of being brash, and most of the time, ruthless.

For now, Lilith wanted Omer to feel safe and happy.

It was much more fun to break them that way.

When they had boarded the helicopter, the boy stared out the windows with wide eyes, taking in the beautiful views of the ocean.

Once her island came into view, her house taking up the majority of the ten acres, Omer whispered in awe.

The only other land within view was uninhabited, full of overgrown trees and shrubbery.

The two-story house, concrete and colored black, was built to withstand weather. The metal roofing, also black, was hard to spot in the dark, appearing more like a shadow than a structure. Very few windows lined the building.

Outdoors was a pool, its blue color lit by several lights, shone like a beacon for the helicopter's landing pad.

Luckily the island was only a two-hour travel by boat, which allowed her to hire a helicopter pilot from the mainland when she chose to bring the helicopter pilot to her island. Many times she used her yacht to visit the mainland, but majorly gave those duties to Leo when they needed supplies.

Or, other times, he hired people to do the task for him, if Lilith needed him by her side. Unless she was in the states, Leo was always nearby, even if he was out of sight. The bodyguard was well compensated for his dedication and loyalty.

"I get to spend a year here?" Omer asked as Leo gathered the boy's belongings. Everything he owned fit in one medium sized bag. "I love to swim. I learned in the ocean and have never been in a pool before."

"I'm sure there will be time for that," Lilith assured him. "When you're not working."

When Omer asked of his job responsibilities, Lilith gave a vague blanket statement. "Whatever I require of you."

"Lady, for what you're paying, I'd do anything."

That was exactly what she wanted to hear.

Except for the way he called her 'lady'.

Soon, she would teach him how to address her properly.

For now, she wanted him under the illusion that this would be a satisfying job. It was more fun this way.

Welcome

    The chef and maid were instructed to be awake upon their arrival to the island. In a day or two, she would send them back to their own homes, but for now they stayed in the staff building behind her home. It was easier that way, instead of making them ferry to and from the mainland.

    This was another way she wanted Omer to feel welcome and 'at home', for now.

    The chef asked what Omer would like to eat, the four large refrigerators and freezers containing anything and everything that Lilith desired on a whim. Steak, hamburger, chicken, and pork were among the many items.

    The maid took the boy's bag from Leo, and carried it to his room.

In contrast to the dark exterior of the home, the walls were white, making the open floor plan on the ground level appear much larger than its three-thousand square feet. The twelve-foot high ceiling also contributed to how open everything felt.

The upstairs was different, where Omer's bedroom was, but Lilith wasn't ready to show him that.

"While she prepares your meal, would you like to go for a swim?"

Omer followed Lilith outside, Leo lurking behind like a third wheel.

Before the boy had a chance to speak, Lilith stripped down to her birthday suit, the blue pool lights reflecting off her toned and lithe body. Quickly, she jumped into the water, but knew it was enough to tease any male, especially a younger male in his hormonal peak.

Revealing how shy he was, Omer sat in one of the expensive lounger chairs, his hands in his lap to cover the bulge in his clothing.

"I thought you wanted to swim," Lilith stated matter-of-factly, only her head above the water. "Don't you want to jump in?"

Not knowing how to reply, Omer looked to Leo for answers. The bodyguard looked out of place in his black slacks and black polo shirt by the glowing pool.

"Don't look at me, boy-oy," Leo exaggerated the way he called him out of name. "She invited you. Not me."

Omer's cheek flushed red, embarrassed. "I'm hungry. Maybe I should eat first?"

Not shy in the least, Lilith took her time walking out of the zero-entry pool. The way the moistness of her flesh gleamed in the blue lights brought out her slight curves.

Seemingly coming out of nowhere, Omer watched as the maid draped a white robe around his new boss.

Still uncomfortable, he kept his hands on his lap.

Lilith approached him, swaying her hips as she walked, the robe hanging open in the front. One of her nipples peeked out of the cloth. "Oh yeah, you'll be a fun one. I can already tell. Let me ask. Are you shaved, like me?" Then she opened the lower part of the robe, allowing the boy's eyes to linger on her smooth pubic mound.

"Uh, um," Omer found it hard to speak. "No, I'm not."

"Waxing. We'll put that on the list for tomorrow. How's that sound?"

Still unable to speak, Omer was relieved when a plate was carried out to him, complete with utensils and a cloth napkin.

"Enjoy your meal," Lilith said, sauntering off into the house. "I need to go wash off. Unless you care to join me."

The boy didn't move, and once again looked at Leo.

"Boy-oy, you don't have a clue what you're in for, do you? Enjoy it while you can."

Coming from Leo's baritone voice, it sounded more like a warning or a threat than words of wisdom or advice.

His appetite had dissipated, but Omer ate anyway. Slowly, he chewed, deep in thought.

Leo was unmoving, standing nearby.

"Is this a sex job?" the boy asked the bodyguard.

"Boy-oy, it's a whatever she wants job. Don't worry, she'll let you know."

++++++

Moments later, a fully dressed Lilith came outside, but didn't acknowledge Omer. Instead, she whispered something in Leo's ear and scampered back inside.

"Looks like the boss is tired and wants me to show you to your room, Your good room." Leo led the boy upstairs.

"Good room? What's that mean?"

"I guess it means you were a good boy today," Leo answered as he opened a door.

Inside was a large bed with an extra thick mattress, plenty of pillows, and plush bedding. On top was Omer's bag of belongings.

Leo pointed. "Your bathroom is through that door."

As Omer entered, Leo shut the door behind him and locked it from the outside.

The boy heard a click, but wasn't aware yet that he had been locked inside. He was still tired and somewhat confused, but jumped on the bed and allowed the multiple pillows to surround his body. It was soft, very comfortable, and shortly after he fell asleep.

Wake

When Omer woke, his bedroom door was wide open.

Leo was standing in the doorway, his arms crossed, watching the boy. "You're asked to shower before you come downstairs. There are many toiletries in there. Get yourself cleaned up. I'll wait."

Not giving it a second thought, Omer complied.

Once he came out of the bathroom, new clothing was laid out on the bed for him.

Leo stood and watched him as he slipped into the plaid Bermuda shorts with his back turned to him. The boy was careful not to drop the towel from around his waist until he had already stepped into the shorts on the floor. In a hurry, he pulled them up to cover himself.

"Trust me, you don't have anything I've never seen," Leo said coldly. "I'll see it plenty while you're here."

The boy reached for the shirt, v-neck, and pulled it over his head. "Yellow? I never dress like this."

"She's paying you to dress however she wants you dressed. She's awaiting you." Leo gestured with both hands for the boy to walk in front of him, and verbally guided him down the stairs.

"Aren't you scrumptious?" Lilith asked as soon as her new employee placed his feet on the first floor. "I could eat you up. First, here's your banking statement. I had Leo run to town this morning. This verifies the payment has been sent to you. See, here's your name, your account number. Everything is now in order."

Omer looked at the paper, counting all the zeros. Two hundred fifty thousand American dollars added more zeros to his currency than he had ever laid his eyes on.

"I see you like that?" Lilith asked. "I'm sorry that you don't have access to the internet to verify, but you'll just have to trust me."

"I didn't even think of that-" Omer started to say before being silenced by her finger across his lips.

"Shh. Okay, your first job is to wax. Well, I'll do the waxing. You just have to lie here," she waved her hands over a massage table. "Breakfast after."

"Wax?"

"Strip down," Lilith patted the table. "Lie on your back. This is all that is required from you."

"Strip down?"

"Are you a parrot? Get naked."

This being the first time that his boss had used a sharp tone with him threw Omer off guard. His cheeks reddened as he slowly lowered his shorts, but he complied. Using both hands, he covered his genitalia.

With grace and charm, she outstretched her arm, gently grasping Omer's hand. "Lie on your back. So easy. This is all I ask of you."

He did as instructed, but it was obvious Omer was still uncomfortable by the way his hands covered his crotch. Leo laughed, but it went ignored. Lilith didn't seem to mind his interruption.

"The wax is still warming. You do know, you'll have to uncover for this, right? Do I need to tie you down? If not, place your arms by your side."

Leo stepped forward, making everyone more aware of his presence.

"I'm sorry, lady, it's just I don't know what's happening."

With the speed of a jackal, Lilith whipped her head towards her employee. "I'm not lady. I'm your boss, and you'll address me as such."

Leo chuckled.

"Sorry, boss," Omer muttered.

"I'll put hot wax on your pubic hair. Then I'll put a strip over it. When I pull away the strip, it will rip your hair from the roots, leaving you hairless in that region."

Omer tried to sit up, but Leo was quick to pin his shoulders down with force. "The boss asked you to lie on your back."

It was Lilith's turn to laugh. "I get waxes myself. You saw how polished I keep my feminine area. There's nothing to worry about."

Before applying the hot substance, Lilith used her fingers and petted his pubic hair like she was petting a dog. Smooth, slow, sensual strokes with the tips of her fingers which were meant to excite the boy. "So bushy. Thick. Dark. Natural."

His flaccid penis responded by stiffening and standing up at attention.

"Oh, this will be fun," Lilith remarked.

And Wax

"I see you like that?" Lilith questioned her subject.

Slowly, she dipped a birchwood stick into the hot, sticky wax. Her eyes remained on the boy's private area, while the popsicle stick collected the heated substance. "Have you ever heard that beauty is painful?"

Omer tried to sit up again, and Leo was quick to hold him down by his shoulders. "Boy-oy, what did she tell you? Do you want to be tied down?"

"Are you serious?" Omer's lower lip quivered and his stiffened member slowly deflated. "Painful? Tie me down? Is this necessary?"

With a flick of her eyes, Lilith looked at Leo, and the bodyguard nodded. Their silent conversation, completely understood by the both of them.

Not in a hurry, wanting this moment to last, Lilith rubbed the wax on the lateral part of the dark pubic bush. She matted it down, to ensure that section of hair was fully coated, all the way to his skin.

Leo prevented the boy from jumping off the table.

Omer screamed a curse word loudly.

When his legs kicked, Lilith demanded Leo strap him down. The leather was hanging from the table, ready to be latched over the boy's shoulders and knees.

"I may have overheated the wax." Lilith stated this as a fact and not an apology. "Still, it's required. For the job."

"No!" Omer screamed, but he was no match for Leo. "Please. Not this."

"If you can't handle this, you shouldn't have applied for the job. Don't you recall saying you'd do anything for money?" Lilith touted as she placed a cotton strip over the too-hot wax.

The way the boy's body shook beneath her touch pleased her. His hips tried to wiggle, but due to the restraints, there was nowhere for him to move.

Once the strip was pressed firmly against his body, and well covered with wax, Lilith snapped her wrist, pulling it away from the boy's crotch.

Omer howled like a wounded animal.

In her hand, Lilith admired all the curled pubes that had been lifted at the roots. "Oh, it may be too hot. Is this some skin?"

Leo noticed the red patch of the boy's body, now hairless, but colored ruby, from where the skin had also detached. It was the same exact size as the cotton strip held in his boss' hand. "Yeah, that appears to be an angry wound."

"Angry wound?" Omer asked. "Please, no more. Stop!"

"You work for me, boy," Lilith reminded him. "You need to be hairless."

The strips were a couple inches in width, and this time when she applied the wax, it coated the side of his flaccid penis. "This will be fun."

The strip didn't lay flat against his body, and raised with a lump where it also covered his male member.

This time when she pulled the strip away, his penis raised with it, her eyes staring at how quickly it jumped up. She swore she saw the skin tear free. It was like pulling away a band-aid, but covered in industrial strength adhesive. "Look, more skin! And hair!"

To prove what she had said, Lilith showed the cotton strip to Leo. "Look, right here, that might even be some blood?"

"Yes," Leo said, as he inspected the boy's crotch. "His pecker looks like an overcooked hot dog. One side of it is swollen and bloody. Not dripping blood, but on the surface. But there is no hair there."

With tears in his eyes, Omer begged for the woman to stop. "C'mon, you can't do this to me."

"Can't?" Lilith mocked. "Can't? I do not know that word. I'll teach you to tell me what I can and can't do."

This time, when she applied the wax, she covered the entire bottom of his penis, scrotum to head. For a cheap thrill, she used her palm to grip his sex organ. The cotton formed to it like a second layer of flesh. "No erection now?"

One hand held the mushroomed head close to his body, her other the bottom of the strip near his scrotum. When she pulled, Omer's body flinched and tears wet his cheeks. It ripped away with an audible ripping sound.

When released, the penis fell to the side, newly exposed under layers of tender pain making contact with his body. From the top view, other than the leaking fluids, the penis looked intact, dangling limply.

The white cotton strip was red with blood.

"Did he have hair there?" Leo asked. "I didn't see any hair. I do see lumps of… What would you call that? I know it's flesh, but it looks more like oatmeal that's been dyed."

Omer raised his head, trying his best to look at his crotch.

"You'll see it later, honey," Lilith warned. "Let's just say it looks ruined. Like Leo said, a busted open hot dog, covered with ketchup. How long until you think the skin grows back. Or will it? Untie him."

The pain in Omer's face was obvious, so Leo unstrapped him with a warning, "Attack her, or me. I dare you."

The boy groaned as he sat up, his legs dangling off the side of the table.

His eyes lingered on what used to be his most favorite part of his anatomy. He raised his body part to find that blisters lined the damaged section of the penis, them leaking clear fluids. Since the skin had been removed, and the way it laid atop his scrotum painted that red. "No! No!"

"Typical response," Leo said, on guard, standing directly in front of the boy.

"Now, masturbate for me," Lilith smirked.

Omer looked at her in anger. "What? No. I can't. Are you crazy?"

Standing behind him, Lilith reached her arm around his waist and grabbed it. The penis didn't stiffen, but she stroked it, up and down. Slowly, softly, sensually, but with a firm grasp.

Reflexes kicked in, and Omer raised his elbow, an attempt to loosen his boss' grip. Instead, she grabbed harder, her fingernails deeply embedded into the sex organ.

His elbow eventually connected with her ribs, knocking her backwards, but her fingernails pulled away thicker masses of penis flesh, and dragged themselves up his shaft. Blood and chunks of meat stuck beneath her fingernails. Larger wounds opened. Blisters burst open wider.

Leo drew back a fist. "You've messed up now, boy-oy." His fist connected with the boy's nose, knocking him out instantly as blood dripped down his face.

"This will be fun," Lilith said, rubbing the tender spot of her ribs from the boy's boney elbow.

Teaching the Job

Omer woke on a couch in the downstairs living area, Leo hunched over him and breathed his hot breath in the boy's face.

Instantly, Omer was aware that he was still undressed. The agony in his crotch throbbed immensely.

"He's awake," the body guard alerted Lilith.

"Great," her voice cooed from a distance. "My sweet Omer. How are you feeling."

"His eyes are darting around the room. Like a wounded animal ready to attack. I hope he does," Leo ended with a chuckle.

"Give him a break," Lilith's voice neared. "He's had a hard day at work."

Trying to sit upright inflamed Omer's suffering.

"No, boy-oy, stay there." Leo's voice was loud and thunderous.

Out of the corner of his eye, Omer saw Lilith, holding something, but he couldn't make out what it was.

She knelt, her knees buried in her plush carpet, eyeing his injuries. Lilith reached out, and placed something on the boy's crotch that sent radiating pains throughout his body.

Omer's body tightened. "Please! Stop!"

"It's just an ice bag, darling," Lilith applied pressure to the item, smashing his cock flat as a pancake. "I realize I may have botched that wax job. My bad."

"Your bad?" What is this?" Omer tried to swat the ice bag away, but Leo grabbed his wrist.

"I could snap this boney thing like a twig. Give the word boss."

"No, he's new. And maybe I am at some fault." Her words were kind, but her actions weren't. She lifted the ice bag and used a long fingernail to poke into a blister that hadn't yet burst. The largest one ruptured like an explosion of spouting water and pus.

"Stop! No more!"

Lilith's voice changed, becoming deeper and authoritative. "I was going to be nice and give you breakfast. You'd have to make it yourself. I've sent the staff away. But with that attitude, I'm thinking of sending you to your room."

The night before, Omer remembered that Leo had told him that he was going to 'his good room'. The thought of that didn't sound bad. "Can I go home? Please?"

"Home? You have a job to do," Lilith quickly reminded him.

"This is no job. Why are you doing this to me?"

"Who knows? Boredom? Power? Fun. I like to get my kicks in ways that others don't understand. Why watch someone else's imagination in a movie? Why read an author's fiction? I prefer to create my own fun, unscripted. Each character responds differently, and that amuses me. You can't go home, but you can go to your bad room."

Her words made Leo laugh out loud. "Yeah, I vote for that. That'll whip him into shape."

"Bad room? What's that?" Tears now feel down Omer's face. 'Please. What if I quit the job?"

"You can quit anytime. But that's bad for you. Or you can stay another three hundred and sixty-four days. That's good for you. Ask Leo, he knows."

"Yeah. She made me everything that I am," Leo chimed in, proud of himself. "I travel the world. Have fun. I want for nothing. Lots of perks of the job."

"Rewards for loyalty. See?"

Nothing was making sense to Omer.

"I'll give the money back," Omer begged. "Please."

"We're getting nowhere with him. I vote for the bad room," Leo looked at Lilith. "That's one of the perks of the job I really enjoy."

"Okay. He's new. Probably hungry. That's punishment right there," Lilith agreed. "Twelve hours. No food, and sent to the punishment room."

Leo didn't have to be told what to do. His large fingers spread across Omer's neck, squeezing hard enough to cut off the oxygen. "Upstairs now. I dare you to fight me."

Stunned, Omer complied. Every step he took bounced his scrotum off his thigh, a reminder of his pain. His gut instincts informed him that his scrawnier frame was no match for Leo's muscular build, but he knew he had to try. Using his elbows as weapons again, he swung them backwards into Leo's rib cage.

Two blows connected, one on each side, but it only made Leo tighten his fingers around the boy's neck.

Before Omer knew what was happening, Leo threw him on his back, supine laid awkwardly on the stairs, each one digging into different parts of his vertebrae.

"Boy-oy! You think you can hurt me? Nope! Wrong!" Leo choked him, depriving the boy of oxygen, until his victim fell unconscious.

The Punishment Room

When Omer came to, he found himself lying on a cold, hardwood floor. The walls were barren. Other than his body, the only other object in the room was a bucket. The lights were bright, so bright that they burned his eyes.

With a hand, he shielded his face, and saw there was writing on the wall. Red and sloppy large letters. 'USE THE BUCKET OR EAT YOUR OWN MESS'.

"What is this?" Omer stood, and ran his fingers across the red paint.

There was a glass window, blacked out, and a door without a knob. After running his fingers along the lines of the door frame, he realized the door was locked and impossible to open.

Then he tried the window.

The plastic bucket was the only item he had to try and bust the glass, and several attempts of slamming it against the glass proved the glass was stronger than the plastic. A thin line cracked in the side of the bucket.

Omer began thinking out loud. "Even if I get out of this room, I have to get past Leo. Even then, I'm trapped on an island. How far can I swim?"

"He's awake!" Leo's voice came from above.

There were speakers flush with the ceiling, the speaker grill being the only visible part. Light appeared on the other side of the window, and Omer saw another room. The glass wouldn't have been an exit to the outside even if he had busted it open.

Leo stood behind Lilith, and the woman slowly swayed her body, while she unbuttoned her shirt.

"Touch yourself, Omer," she beckoned to him.

The woman wore no bra, but her artificial breasts didn't need to be held up by fabric. They were firm and perfectly placed by a skilled doctor. Her large nipples turned into buds as she caressed herself.

"No!" he screamed. "Let me out! You can't do this!"

"Honey, I can do anything I want." Lilith lowered her yoga pants, turning her back towards the boy, her back arched, her buttocks exposed. Between the diamond-shaped opening of her thighs, her pink slit glistened in the bright lights. "Touch yourself, Omer!"

"No! It hurts!"

"Touch me, Leo," she turned to the side.

Leo approached her from behind like a dog in heat, sticking himself inside of her.

"You're both sick!" Omer screamed. "Let me out of here!" His flat hands pounded on the glass.

"It's bulletproof, idiot," Leo said through a smile, still humping his boss.

"He's a buzz kill. Push the button, Leo."

Omer watched as Leo touched a part of the wall below the window, a part of the wall he couldn't see.

Music blared loudly, causing Omer to cover his ears with his hands. Fast tempo, low tuned guitars blared. Each time a drum played, Omer swore that he felt the room shake. Even when he tried to scream, he couldn't hear himself over the loud noise.

Strobe lights rotated. Super bright. Darkness. Super bright. Darkness.

Watching his boss and her bodyguard through the glass was confusing. Leo thrust himself harder, deeper, and faster into Lilith to beat with the music.

Eventually they tired, and waved goodbye through the glass.

Omer screamed until his throat was raw. He kept his eyes shut to try to ignore the strobing lights, but the bright white was too much and creeped through his eyelids.

Then the room got cold.

So cold that Omer could see his own breath when it was on the white light.

Not knowing what else to do, Omer curled into a fetal position, hugging his legs to his chest. He sunk his face into the crook of his arm to block the light and tried covering his ears again with both hands. It was no use. The music was so loud his body was vibrating.

His ruined crotch flared with pain, seemingly hot compared to the frigid temperature.

Between not eating and the intrusive sounds, his headache began minutes into his punishment. Minutes felt like hours.

Almost every sense of Omer's was under attack. Sight, sound, and touch (loud music, strobe light, cold temps) were bad enough. His sense of smell wasn't invaded until his bladder urged him to use the restroom. Omer held it for as long as he could, but it became an urgent need.

The writing on the wall, the warning that if he didn't use the bucket he would be forced to eat his own waste, lingered in his mind.

It took several attempts of stumbling to reach the plastic bucket, and the intervals of blinding light and darkness made it almost impossible for him to aim his urine stream.

Between the combination of his misery and the pain of his penis, he had long forgotten the crack in the bucket.

The bright light only lasted a second or two, but he knew he saw his liquid waste leaking onto the hardwood floor.

He wished he would be let out of the room very soon, but also hoped it would be long enough for his urine to dry, just in case Lilith forced him to lick it up like the words on the wall warned.

He also recalled how Lilith told him his punishment would last twelve hours.

In his current situation, half a day would feel like an eternity.

Not only was his body being tortured, so was his mind. This would be more than enough to drive any sane person wild.

The only happy thought he could muster was the bank statement she had showed him earlier that morning. Technically, he was much richer than he ever dreamt imaginable for someone like him. The only problem was surviving the year the job required.

Before they let him out, Omer knew the money wasn't worth it.

Niceties

"Times up!" Leo screamed through the open door.

The light was constant and solid, but Omer's vision hadn't adjusted. He still saw strobes. The music was off, but it still played in his head. His body had become accustomed to the cold by numbing itself.

His punishment may have been complete, literally, but it didn't feel like it.

"Huh?" A cloud of smoke proved it was still cold in the room. "What?"

"C'mon," Leo waved a hand towards himself. "You're out. Now play nice. Okay? It was only twelve hours. You're one of the lucky ones. You didn't even have to use the bucket. Bowel movements can be a pain."

That was when Omer saw that the bucket was empty. Either his urine dried up, or it all leaked out and he had done a good job of placing the bucket over the spill. He hadn't had food in what felt like forever, but maybe that was a good thing that he hadn't voided his bowels in the bucket.

"What a shame," Lilith came up from behind Leo, holding a blanket, spreading her arm span. "Let's get you warmed up. It's cold in there. Shame about the bucket. I enjoy making them clean that up."

"Huh?"

"Go get the sweet boy, Leo. He's stuck or something."

Leo made a *brrr* sound to acknowledge the cold, but stepped in the room, and grabbed Omer by both arms. "Stand up. You're okay now. She's letting you know the job. But if you displease her, you'll be back in here. I've done it. Made me the man I am today."

Omer's head was still swimming, but he allowed Leo to lead him out of the room.

Lilith wrapped him in the blanket, and gave him a motherly hug, gentle and with a concerned look on her face. "You'll warm up soon. I made you some dinner. Well, Leo did. Would you like a drink? Cocktails always make me feel better."

The way they were guiding Omer, it felt like he was floating through space and time, his mind still numb and confused from the punishment room. They ushered him to the downstairs couch, wrapped snug in the warm blanket. They left him alone, neither of his captors in view.

Leo was in the kitchen behind him, making a plate of food.

Lilith was at the bar, pouring drinks.

Finding enough strength to break through his mental barrier of a hazed mind, Omer finally spoke. "I'll give the money back."

Lilith approached, ice cubes clinking against the edges of the glasses. She tried to hand one to Omer, but the boy only stared at her. After setting his drink on the table next to him, she studied him. A thin glaze of moisture coated his eyes.

"Huh? Interesting. Nobody has ever volunteered to do this job for free."

Her words cut him like a knife, but not physically. The slice was made to his fragile mind. "No. I mean…"

Leo had a plate of food, this time with plastic cutlery. "Have you not learned anything? Keep this up and you'll go back into the punishment room."

"No!" Omer lashed out, trying to stand up, but his legs failed him. His knees went weak and bent, forcing him to sit back down. "Never! Please, I'll do anything to not ever go back in there!"

"That's what I wanted to hear," Lilith said, taking a sip. "That's the spirit. Eat the food. Drink your drink. Then we'll speak."

Leo and Lilith both left the room, Omer's eyes following them.

He wasn't sure where they went. Like an owl with his head on a swivel, Omer surveyed the room. They were gone. Deep inside, he knew that they couldn't have gone far. It was still a relief that he wasn't in their presence.

In fear that they would soon return, Omer took a bite of chicken, which was now cold. The drink burned his throat, and the moment the alcohol hit his nearly empty stomach, he wanted to vomit.

His airway closed, his abdominal muscles contracted. His esophagus felt like it was climbing backwards, out of his throat. Omer heaved, but there was nothing in his body to upchuck. A bit of dried saliva foam filled his mouth.

Omer heard laughter.

They were out of sight, but he knew they were laughing at him. He knew they were watching him. On top of all his negative feelings, paranoia sunk in.

His last order had been to eat and drink. His body tried to reject it, but terror of being forced back into the punishment room gave him the resolve to do as he was instructed.

Chewing the cold, rubbery chicken wasn't easy, but he forced himself. The third bite made his empty belly feel full. The alcoholic beverage was something he couldn't force down his gullet, no matter how many times he tried.

Soon, Omer fell asleep, sitting upright.

New Duties

Omer woke up in the same position as when he fell asleep. His aching bladder was in dire need of being emptied.

Leo sat in a chair across from him. "Good. You're awake. It's a brand-new day."

"Bathroom?" It was a single word, posed as a question, asking permission.

Leo sat back and smiled. "Sure."

Omer stood, not noticing the heavy weight around his ankle. It was when he tried to take a step that he felt the chain, keeping him in place, attached under the couch. He shoved the blanket off his lower body, and saw a thick shackle with a lock attached.

"Darling," Lilith appeared out of nowhere. "We couldn't have you running amok while we slept. Give him the key, Leo."

After unlocking himself, Leo followed him to the bathroom. "You really shouldn't have attacked me or the boss. Now my orders are to stay with you. At all times."

Lilith even followed, and Omer felt like he was on display. They didn't allow him to close the bathroom door, and both stood in the doorway. If his bladder hadn't been so full, it would have been difficult for him to start a stream. But he did, and they both watched.

A few drips of the acidic bodily waste burned his injured penis, and he moaned in pain. It made Leo laugh. More blisters had burst, creating tender pockets of pain lining his shaft. Two fingers gently cradled his member to not apply any pressure on the open wounds.

"Your breakfast is what you left from last night," Lilith informed him. "You will return to the couch. Eat and drink. Until it's all gone."

If Omer had more strength, maybe he would have tried to fight. Tried to get away. Even if he did, he would still be stuck on the island. The tides of the water would make it impossible to swim to safety. Unless there was a nearby boat, he was hopeless. "Yes, boss."

"He is learning," Leo said with a shrug. "You're right."

++++++

Still under Leo's watchful eye, Omer ate the chicken that was now crusty from sitting out all night.

The beverage had been watered down by the melted ice cubes, but even the smell of alcohol burned Omer's nostrils. Forcing himself, he took a sip. "What is this drink?"

"Vodka and piss," Leo said, comfortable enough to lean back in a plush chair. "Hers, not mine."

The same familiar feeling of being sick made Omer's body flush with heat. In a hurry, Omer ran back towards the toilet, making Leo jump out of his chair.

The sounds of the boy retching filled the silent house.

Small chunks of chicken floated in the toilet bowl, some sticking to the sides.

"And I sent the maid home," Lilith said from behind him. "You're cleaning that up."

Omer wiped his mouth. "Where's the cleaning supplies?"

"That's a good boy," Lilith patted the top of his head, same as she would a dog. "You don't need supplies. You have a tongue. You're not leaving this room until my toilet is sparkling white."

"What?"

"You heard her!" Leo screamed as he shoved Omer's head in the water that hadn't been flushed yet.

Lilith tapped her bodyguard lightly on the shoulder. "Don't drown him. Let him up."

When Omer raised his head, lumps of chewed-up chicken stuck to his cheeks. Discolored, brownish water dripped from his chin. Barf lodged in his eyebrows and dripped into his eyelashes.

Maid Duties

"You were hired to be a houseboy and agreed to do whatever was asked of you. The maid is gone, you made the mess. Now you clean it up. Flush the toilet, then begin." Lilith looked at her wrist for effect, even though she wasn't wearing a watch. "You have ten minutes."

Omer was perched on his knees, staring into a white porcelain bowl. The swirling water making its way down the drain may have washed away the bulk of the sick mess, but smaller lumps clung to the sides of the bowl.

There was even a brown mark on the bottom, which Omer assumed to be from a bowel movement, but couldn't be for certain. He tried to tell himself that he didn't recall it being there earlier. Anything to believe it was vomited up food and not from someone's rectum.

The threat of Leo drowning him felt real.

His stomach had already expunged the entirety of its contents, but that didn't prevent the dry heaves.

"Times running out, boy-oy," Leo whispered in his ear, bent down to his level. "You have a choice. You could go back to the punishment room."

Omer forced himself to crane his neck and twist his head into the bowl. When he stuck out his tongue and touched it to the porcelain, it was cold, and he closed his eyes and imagined he was licking an ice cream cone.

"Seven more minutes," Lilith reminded him.

Where Omer licked had felt smooth, but then his tongue came across something that felt textured. He opened his eyes to see what it was. He couldn't be sure, but it was either partially digested chicken or stomach bile.

Opening his eyes was the worst thing he could have done.

His stomach may have been empty, but its lining churned, producing newly discovered contents. Foamy, yellow, globs of moisture discharged through his nose and his mouth.

"I can't! I can't do it!" Omer cried out, his voice bouncing back in his ears, echoing off the water.

Lilith motioned to Leo, who once again wrapped his hands around the boy's neck, dunking him into the shallow water.

The foamy stuff invaded his open eyes and burned them.

His lungs gasped for oxygen, and his open mouth sucked in water and vomit.

His body was even too weak to fight.

His neck went limp, like he had given up.

"Let him up, Leo."

"Just kill me now. I can't do this!" Omer pleaded. "Death would be better than this!"

"Leo," Lilith said, as she walked away. "I'm bored with him. Put him back in the room until I figure out what to do with him. He's weak. I have no use for him."

Leo raised his eyebrows. "Are you sure, boss? It's only a couple of days in. You can still break him. I'm sure of it."

"Do I pay you to question me? Do I pay you to think? Do as I say. I can come up with other plans. Better plans."

The bodyguard knew better than to speak. His employer was mad, and he knew that when she was mad, it was best to not be in her way. Best to not even be in the same room as her.

Lilith thumbed through her phone, and dialed. "Mr. Axel, my current employee isn't working out. What else do you have for me?"

Change of Employee

On the Home Front

"Man oh man! She's taking an American employee!" Axel's excitement was contagious through the phone.

"What?" Terrence said in confusion. "I thought she already picked another one."

"Yeah, she did. But she doesn't like him. She wants me to come pick him up and see him home safely. She also wants you to come. Draw up new paperwork or something."

"Hmm mm," the lawyer said thoughtfully, chewing on the end of his pen. "That's peculiar. She's never done that before. What kind of spell did you cast on her? You're young and handsome. That seems to do something to her."

Axel ignored the insult that was disguised as a compliment. "I have my concerns about going to her island. She kinda gives me the creeps, but if you're with me, then it's all good, right?"

"Oh yeah. I've been to her island on several occasions."

Axel remembered that Lilith had mentioned knowing the lawyer intimately. It made sense that Terrence had visited the island. "This is what you hired me for? Right? Does that mean I get that bonus you dangled in front of my face?"

"Sure. This is what I've been waiting for. I -er, uh- we, can bring her down. She's always loved the fact that she's untouchable. She's getting sloppy. If she does take an American employee, our country is more likely to try and prosecute her. If not, the publicity would be bad for her family."

"She's sending her plane for us tonight. Does that work for you?"

"Lilith is the kind of woman, that when she beckons, I go. You do know she pays me hourly, right? Well above the bar of my normal pay."

Welcomed

"You sure pull out all the stops, Lily," Terrence said as gave her a kiss on her cheek. His mouth was aiming for hers, but she turned her head. When his lips missed its mark, he was disappointed.

"I trust your flight and helicopter ride was sufficient?" Lilith was absolutely glowing in her flowing, white caftan. The material was thin, sheen, and see through, revealing her black string bikini underneath. She pulled away from Terrence's embrace and reached for Axel. Her hand laid gently on the back of his neck, and pulled his face into hers.

Lightly, she pressed her lips to his, and let the contact linger a few moments. "How are you, Axe?"

Surprised by her public display of affection and nickname, Axel took a step back. "Everything was great. I slept a good part of the ride."

"I'm working on my tan," she replied, laying back down in the lounger near the pool.

An umbrella covered her chair, providing shade, which would make it impossible to tan, but neither man said anything to contradict her statement.

Sweat rolled down the lawyer's face and he regretted wearing his suit, complete with jacket and tie. "I wrote up the necessary contract. From what Axel's told me, you are firing your current employee and taking another?"

"All business with you? That's something I used to appreciate. Now it bores me. If you want a drink, you know where the bar is. You do plan on staying the night before the long journey home, aren't you?"

"Where's Leo?" Terrence asked.

"Leo? Who's that?" Axel chimed in. "I thought his name was Omer?"

"My bodyguard," she said softly, raising her empty glass. "He's around. Tending to Omer. Axel, would you be a dear and go pour me a vodka sour? Heavy on the vodka, light on the sour mix. Everything you need is on the bar. Right inside, take a left. Can't miss it."

Inside the sliding glass door, Axel felt like he was surrounded with luxury. Plush carpeting and couches. He couldn't believe how soft the flooring was and how it felt like he was walking on a cloud. Art decorated the walls, too abstract to be anything significant, gave the appearance of money.

"Your house. It's stunning," Axel observed, sticking his head back outside. There was no reply. The lawyer was seated next to Lilith, his back bent and whispering in Lilith's ear. They were deep in conversation, and not paying him any attention.

It hadn't occurred to Axel that he was still holding his overnight bag, and wasn't sure where to place it. He felt like an intruder, with it being the first time in the home and his host wasn't with him. The bar was exactly where she said it would be. It was made of glass, with shelving beneath it. Many different types of liquor were on display.

"I'll get that," a loud voice came from behind. Leo came to the bottom of the stairs, his black tank top showcasing his thick shoulders and biceps. "Vodka sour? Right? I think that was her choice today."

"Uh, yeah," Axel said, and tried to hand his bag to the man.

Leo walked right past him. "I meant I'll get her a drink. Put the bag anywhere. Do I look like a bellhop?"

"Uh, okay. You must be Leo?"

"What gave it away?" The bodyguard was busy pouring and didn't make an attempt for eye contact.

"Well, I thought I saw you back in New York at the restaurant, but we weren't introduced. Terrence asked about you outside, so I figured it out."

"That stupid rat bastard is here? He actually showed up?"

Technically, this was a job for Axel, and he couldn't come up with a professional response to the remark, so he ignored the honest opinion. "They're by the pool."

"I'm aware. I'm always aware of her whereabouts," Leo boasted, carrying the single glass out of the sliding glass door. "Pour your own drink. Make yourself whatever you want."

"Awkward," Axel said to nobody but himself.

Friendships?

When Leo came out with the drink, Terrence stood to greet the man, his arm extended for a handshake.

Leo set the drink down, but didn't take the lawyer's hand. The muscular man stood behind Lilith's lounge chair, his hands crossed between his hips.

"Leo, is that any way to greet our company? Terrence is here on business. That's all." Lilith raised the glass to her mouth. "Yummy. Exactly how I like it."

Axel observed, from the glass door, the tension between the lawyer and the bodyguard. When Terrence sat back down, he kept space between himself and Lilith.

Rather than pouring himself a drink, so he could keep a clear head, Axel joined the group outside. Leo's stance made him nervous, so he stood also.

"Why all the tension, boys? Aren't we all friends here?" Lilith asked, her also now standing. "It's hot. I need a dip in the pool. Why doesn't everyone get comfortable?"

All the men's eyes, six in total, watched as she pulled the sheer fabric over her head. The tiny strings of her tiny swimsuit crossed above her slightly protruded hip bones. The small triangles covering the woman parts of her chest and crotch left nothing to the imagination.

Her eyes lingered on Axel as she sashayed her way towards the pool. "Make a drink. Go for a swim with me? You're in paradise. Why not enjoy it?"

"I'm game," Terrence chimed in. "Leo, I'll take a Scotch. I'll be right back. I need to change into my swimwear."

"Make your own drink," Leo said, eyeballing the man from head to toe. "Do I work for you?"

Not wanting to stay outside and make conversation with Leo, Axel followed the lawyer inside the house. "What's up with that?"

"History, that's all. I'm going upstairs," Terrence pointed. "There's a bathroom right there for you to change."

"I thought this was a business trip? Not leisure?" Axel asked.

"We don't leave until the morning. Like she said, we're in paradise. Let's enjoy it."

Something about the lawyer, the way he felt more comfortable than himself, Axel couldn't shake away a bad feeling.

+++++

Terrence and Lilith were in the pool, once again standing close and speaking in hushed voices. For a moment, Axel regretted not joining them, but an internal voice was nagging him to stay alert. Everything felt wrong about this trip.

"Why ya so uptight?" Leo's voice boomed from behind the umbrella providing shade. "You're not getting in?"

Axel shook his head. "Uh, no. Where's Omer?"

"He's fine. In his room. He'll be out for dinner. Let me give you some advice. She likes making people feel welcome. Plays into her illusion that she gets one over on people. Empowered or something. Like a praying mantis. The way the female doesn't bite off her mate's head until after sex."

"Why are you telling me this?"

"So you'll relax a bit."

No matter how hard he tried, breathing easy wasn't something Axel could do until he stepped off the island the next morning.

Dinner

The dining room table was set formally with several utensils next to the plate and cloth napkins. It was a burden that Leo had to assume since the other staff were still away, but at least Lilith granted him permission to dine with them.

"Ravioli. My nanny taught me when I was a kid. It's her special recipe," Leo said as he shoved the napkin into the neck of his shirt. "Hope you all enjoy it. Or not. I really don't care."

"Where are your table manners?" Lilith nagged. "This is a business meeting, and I won't have you ruin it for me."

"Right," Terrence chimed in. "I have the contracts in my briefcase."

"Or we can discuss a change of plans?" Lilith proposed. "Eat and drink. Be merry. Let's talk. Maybe you could extend your trip?"

The lawyer, seated next to her, reached out and laid his hand on top of Lilith's. "As much as I would enjoy that, I really can't. I have obligations at home. But we still have tonight, Lily."

The way Terrence called her by her shortened name sent danger signals through the synapses clicking in Axel's brain. Whatever shared history they had, what he wasn't privy to, made him feel like an outsider.

"I have a toast," Lilith raised her wine glass in the air and clinked her fork lightly on the side. "Or better yet, I'll allow Axel to do the talking."

The lump that formed in Axel's throat refused to budge no matter how hard he swallowed. To try and force it down, he took a drink. "Um, where's Omer?"

"He didn't feel well. Sleeping, I expect," Lilith replied. "Why don't you tell Terrence of your little business venture?"

"Business venture? Why am I just now hearing of this?" Terrence looked puzzled. "You two starting a company or something? Need legal advice?"

"Now? Like this? Right here?" Axel looked even more confused than the lawyer. "You sure?"

"I assure you, everything is fine." Lilith spoke with a stillness.

"Okay, then," Axel began. "I guess you could say we're going into business together."

"Is that so?" Terrence's mouth was full of pasta when he spoke. "What kind?"

"What I always do. Private investigating."

The lawyer shrugged. "Makes sense. That's what you do."

Axel grinned so wide that the curves of his lips raised his cheeks, revealing his bone structure. "It is. For the highest bidder. I did get her to agree to hiring an American."

Terrence paused mid-chew, his mouth still full. First his eyes landed on Axel, then Lilith. "What am I missing here?"

"Axel sold you out. He claimed you were trying to get me arrested or something? Preposterous of you. Did it hurt that much when I ended our relationship? Is this how you'd try to hurt me? Revenge or something?"

Terrence focused directly on Lilith. "He lied to you! You would believe him over me?"

"I thought the same. Until I saw video, and heard recordings. Axel played along to get you here. Sure, you probably would have come if I asked, but I like this way better. It's like a surprise birthday party, but the opposite. Is a surprise death party a thing? Or did I just make that up? You wanted me to take an American, and I'm doing just that. I choose you."

Leo laughed so loud that food flew out of his mouth.

Terrence tried to stand, but his legs felt like jelly, and betrayed him.

"Your wine. Drugged. You'll be asleep very soon."

"You can't do this," Terrence said, now holding his head up with his palms, elbows on the table. "People know I'm here."

"Yes, but your helicopter went down earlier," Lilith continued explaining her plan. "That cost me more money than you could ever imagine to stage, but I'm sure it will pay off. There may even be search parties looking for you. Far away from here, of course."

"What?" Axel's head also started to feel heavy. It was hard to keep his eyes open. "But I was on the helicopter, too."

"Don't be dense. You think I could ever trust you after this? You sold out your own employer. It's a shame that they'll never recover your bodies in the helicopter wreckage. But not a shame for me. I think this will be fun."

Animosity

"I'm so glad you decided to wake up," Lilith said, placing a small peck on Axel's cheek. "I'd hate for you to miss the show."

His head was still foggy, but Axel knew he was in danger. "Show? We had a deal? Remember? A fat paycheck for delivery of the lawyer. I don't understand."

"You made a deal with the devil, and lost. Well, I guess I'm not really THE devil, but some would say I am a devil. Before I'm through with you, you'll understand. Leo!" Lilith called out. "He's awake. I think we're ready."

Axel realized he was in a room that he didn't recognize. This room was small, the walls and ceilings painted black. There was a chill in the air, making him suddenly aware of his own nudity. Thick metal shackles bound his wrists and ankles, connected by chains, attached to the arms and legs of a metal chair.

When Axel raised his hands, he felt something bite into his wrists. Warm blood spilled from fresh wounds and dripped down his palms. "What are these? Razors? On the shackles? Why?" Axel asked. "Why am I tied up? I did what you asked of me."

"I would advise you to not move too much. The blades are a precaution. A learning experience, I suppose. A reminder who is the boss. I'm in charge here, not you."

Leo entered the room, pushing a wheelchair. The lawyer's chin was sunk into the top of his chest. A thick trickle of red dripped from his nose, onto his nude body. Purples on the sides of his face, large bruises, were deep and large, surrounded by cracks in the facial skin.

"Leo got a little out of control with him, as you can see the evidence on his face," Lilith pointed to the wounds.

"This is ludicrous," Axel said, while he eyed the contraptions that were also on the lawyer's wrists and ankles. They were the same as his, but his mind couldn't compute what he was seeing. It was indeed razor blades, lining the handcuffs.

More blood, thicker and dried clots, clung to the lawyer's wrists and ankles.

"One to the chest," Lilith demanded of her bodyguard.

Leo did as instructed, with a balled up fist, and swung it into the lawyer's solar plexus. As the wind was knocked from his lungs, Terrence's body shook involuntarily, his hands flying upwards on the wheelchair arms. The sharp blades faded into the flesh of his joints, connecting hand to arm.

"As you can see, it's very effective," Lilith continued. "If he even thought about fighting back, well, he wouldn't this way."

"How are we doing this?" Leo asked. "If I had it my way, I'd just go ahead and kill him."

"But he doesn't deserve a quick death," Lilith quickly interjected. "Do you think he deserves a quick death, Mr. Axel?"

"What? This wasn't the deal. Why are you doing this?"

Lilith spoke through closed teeth. "Why? Simply because I can. Entertainment. I could use a drink. We'll discuss this downstairs. Leo."

With those words, Lilith and her bodyguard left the room, leaving the two bound men alone.

"What did you do?" Terrence slightly raised his head. "Why? I trusted you. I hired you to put a stop to this."

Axel had no good answer. "We need to get out of here. You know her better than I do. How can we escape?"

"Escape?" Terrence mocked him with a laugh, careful to not move his hands. "You haven't been paying attention, have you? How much did she pay you? What was your price? Just curious, to ease my curiosity. Was it worth it?"

"None of that matters now, does it? We need to put our heads together. We need to figure out something."

"You must really be dense like she said. There's nothing to figure out. You signed our death warrants."

A Show

The glass, looking into the next room, lit up.

Terrence and Axel were helpless in their chairs, bound in place. They could do nothing but watch.

Leo brought Omer into the room on the other side of the window. The employee's eyes were glassed over and barely even blinked. His movements were robotic, like his legs wouldn't bend to his will. There was no fight left in the younger man, and he allowed the bodyguard to place him in front of the window.

Before Lilith came into view, Leo stood behind Omer and threaded his arms through Omer's. The security guard used his biceps to secure Omer's less muscular arms in place.

Leo interlocked his fingers behind Omer's head, his elbows jutted out like wings behind the young boy.

It was then that Lilith was brave enough to stand in front of her victim. The employee was held in place, and still didn't put up a fight.

"What's wrong with him?" Axel asked. "He's like a zombie or something?"

Terrence almost shrugged his shoulders, but stopped himself, in case it would drag his wrists across the razor blades. "Who knows? Drugs maybe? Or a broken will? She likes to break people. It's her game. Thinks it's fun."

"What the-"

Axel stopped speaking mid-sentence and watched as Lilith lowered the boy's short pants. After his clothing was on the ground, Leo placed his feet around the boy's, spread his legs, and used his feet to hold the boy's lower body in place.

If Omer wanted to fight, which it didn't appear that he did, he couldn't due to how he was being held in place. The bodyguard made sure he had a tight grasp on the boy's body.

Lilith dropped to her knees, her face level with the male genitalia.

"Is she going to-"

Once again, Axel's words were cut mid-sentence. His eyes were glued to what had been referred to as 'the show', and it was like watching a train wreck. He couldn't look away.

Lilith used a lover's touch and cupped Omer's scrotum. Her tongue lightly caressed the length of Omer's cock.

There was no other response from her employee, other than his hardened member, sticking straight out from his body at a ninety-degree angle.

"She wants us to watch her suck his dick? What's wrong with it?" Axel asked. "It's practically disfigured. Why in the world? What?"

"Are you getting hard, Axe?" Terrence asked. "Maybe that's what she wants. Maybe this is one of her games."

"Is she going to kill us, or make us her sex slaves?"

The absurdity of Axel's question caused Terrence to shrug his shoulders, and he felt the razor rip into the already tender flesh of his wrist.

Lilith went from sensual to animalistic quickly, her mouth now fully engorged with the boy's penis, in rapid back and forth motions.

When Lilith paused momentarily, she looked directly into the glass window and smiled.

"She's crazy," Axel remarked. "She's getting off on this!"

Lilith's mouth opened wide, lips posed wide, to show her teeth.

Then she took the penis into her face hole, then chomped down with a ferocity.

The two bound men were watching from a side view, and all they could see was Lilith's temples moving on the side of her head like she was grinding her teeth together. Then blood dripped down her chin.

"She just-" Axel started to say, but couldn't complete the sentence.

'Yes, she did," Terrence agreed.

Omer's body quivered. His limbs responded, but Leo's muscles tightened against the boy's resistance. The scream was deafening.

Lilith pulled her face away, her face tethered to his body by a thick string of blood. Bright red coated her lips like lipstick. When she smiled, her ridiculously white teeth were now crimsoned.

Slowly, the woman stood, stared into the glass window, and spit.

A mass of meat, the tip of the mushroomed sex organ, slapped against the glass with a *thud*. It took seconds for it to glide down the viewing window. The severed penis, what was once tightened skin, had now lost its elasticity and spread open like a blooming flower.

A steam of ruby fluid sprayed from Omer's crotch.

Leo laughed.

Proud of herself, Lilith used the back of her hand to wipe away the mess on her face.

She reached for something below the window, something the audience of two couldn't see.

It was small and metal.

It wasn't until a flame spurned from the tip that they realized it was a small-handheld torch.

The flame quieted the blood flow from the divided penis. Red boil bubbles protruded from where Omer's manhood should have been.

This was when Axel forced himself to look away. "She's crazy! Certifiable! She'll kill us!"

"Yeah," Terrence said coldly, his eyes still watching the fire dance on the boy's wound. Dangling bits of meat blackened beneath the blue flame. "Like I said, you did this. I'd love to know what your price was. Was it worth it? Selling me out like this?"

There was no good response, and Axel hadn't realized it, but he was crying, large tears falling down his cheeks. "We have to get out of here! We just have to!"

Axel heard another *thud*, and he forced himself to look again.

Omer's body had fallen to the ground, his hands cupping his absent naughty bits.

Leo and Lilith's laughter, louder than Omer's howls, sent chills down Axel's spine. "I'm so sorry," he cried. "I'm so sorry."

"No, not yet, you aren't," Terrence disagreed. "Soon you'll know the full meaning of sorry."

Stillness

The window went black. The horror show was out of sight, but not out of mind.

Terrence was trying frantically to figure a way out of his wheelchair. Each time he moved his wrists, the chains clattered against the chair's metal frame. The razors did cut into the superficial layers of his wrists, but that was a minor injury compared to what he had just seen. "Axel, are you with me? You have to try!"

The private investigator was pale and stared into an abyss of black window.

"Axel! Stay with me! This is no time to be in shock!" Terrence screamed as loud as he could, but his words weren't registering. The handbrake on the wheelchair was locked in place, but one of his chains must have dislodged it, because his chair rolled forward a bit. "C'mon. We have to try. We can't just sit here!"

"Huh? What?"

"That's it. Snap out of it!" Terrence gritted his teeth through the pain of the razors. With the tiniest of foot movement, he got the chair to roll further. It took some finesse to his strategy, but he eventually rolled into Axel's legs.

Axel finally looked up. "We're dead! She'll torture us! What? What?"

"Calm down. Let's put our heads together and think. There's two of us and only one Leo. We need to come up with something!"

"This is your fault," the first coherent statement dripped from Axel's mouth. "I should be tracking cheating husbands. At home. I never should have taken this job."

"Is that so?" Terrence asked calmly. "My fault? Didn't I warn you? I told you how dangerous she was. But no. You had to get greedy. Take her up on her offer. This is on you!"

Once again, Axel hung his head in shame.

Anger took hold of the lawyer, and he inhaled deeply, conjuring up phlegm from his throat. If his hands were free, he would have beaten the private investigator, but they weren't, so he spit on him instead. The thick mucous projectile landed square on Axel's forehead.

"I deserve that!" Axel screamed. "I'm so sorry."

"Seriously? You're breaking this quick! No. Stay strong. Find that strength!"

Tears continued to fall down Axel's face. "What? You think your words of wisdom will help us now? What's done is done."

The door opened, Leo's large frame a shadow in the doorway. "The greedy one is the weak one. Who would've thunk it?"

Lilith stood behind her bodyguard. "Terrence managed to move his chair, somehow. Go get him. I'd like to have a few words with Axe. Alone."

"No!" Axel's words echoed off the walls of the room. "Please! No! Don't do this to me!"

Leo stood behind the lawyer's chair, and rolled him out of the room.

"No! Get off me, you savage! Let me out of this chair! Fight me like a man!"

Before closing the door, Leo turned around. "You okay alone with him, boss?"

"Yeah. I'm good. It appears that I have a captive audience, literally."

The feeling of dread creeping up Axel's spine took hold of his body, paralyzing him in place. "Please. You don't have to do this."

"You're correct," Lilith acknowledged. "I don't have to do anything. But I do enjoy having fun."

Axel looked up at his captor, shaken by her tranquility. Blood still stained her face from where she bit Omer's penis in half. Her pale skin, in contrast with the darkened gore dried on her face, made her look even more evil.

Then they were alone in the room.

Axel couldn't make himself look at her, in fear of what she would do to him.

Fighting Chances

"You're breaking too soon. No fun for me," Lilith said, hoovering around the bound man. "That's not good. I like a little fight. Mr. Axe, even your name would imply strength. Your rugged exterior. The way you were a tiger in my bed in New York City. What happened?"

"Huh? You think this is a game?" Axel chewed on his lower lip like he was deep in thought. "Why do you do this?"

"For my entertainment mostly. Why does everything need a reason? We could discuss philosophy. Or we can discuss your survival. At this rate, it's a very low percentage." For her own kicks, Lilith rubbed her hand across her captor's thigh.

His body tried to respond by moving away from her touch, but all that did was remind him of the razors on his ankles.

The swelling of his penis betrayed him. Axel's body responded autonomously.

"See, you still have some fight in you. Men are so easy. Tell me what you want, Mr. Axe."

"I want to go home."

"Sum that up. Make it simpler."

"Huh?"

Lilith sighed. "You want to live? Is that simpler? Is that true?"

"Yes."

"And the money?" her words lingered in the air like smoke. "You want money?"

"No! I want my life!"

"But you were willing to sacrifice the lawyer's life in exchange for your greed. Is that true?"

Axel shook his head. "I didn't know you'd kill him. I didn't know you tortured him."

"Hmmmmm. Interesting," Lilith took a step back to examine her subject. "Terrence didn't warn you? He never told you of my proclivities?"

"I guess he did, but-"

"No buts, Mr. Axe. Your own actions landed you here, in my corner of the world. Helpless and bound to a chair. You have nobody to blame but yourself. How does that feel?"

He flicked his eyes upwards. "It doesn't feel good."

"Would you say that makes you angry?"

"Of course."

"Tap into that anger. You might be needing that. What if I told you that you had a chance of walking out of here alive? A little worse for wear, but alive."

It was the first time since dinner that Axel smiled. It was half-hearted, but displayed a glimmer of hope. "What? There's a chance of that?"

"There you go," she said, patting him on his head. "There's that ambition that attracted me to you. Would you kill, to save your own life? What's that theory? Survival of the fittest or something?"

She left the room, leaving Axel alone with his thoughts.

Testing Limits

Leo was equipped with a handgun, standing in the corner of the room. If any of Lilith's victims were to lash out, he would be quick to attack. The threat of a hot bullet, a sudden death, felt very real.

The way the bodyguard pointed the weapon, back and forth between Terrence and Axel, made his boss feel safe.

"Poor Omer here," Lilith said, standing above the boy, now strapped down to a table. "He's still alive. I gave him a little something for the pain because his constant crying was annoying me, but trust me when I say that he can still feel."

The private investigator and the lawyer were also standing, both on opposite ends of the Omer's table. Both of their wrists and ankles were bleeding, and they weren't shackled. It was only the gun that kept them in line.

Axel's movements were slow, but he thought he could get a jump on the evil woman. He thought wrong. His first step towards Lilith and Leo pulled the trigger, creating an ear-splitting boom of a bullet whizzing right past him, lodging in a wall right behind him.

"I never miss," Leo stated. "But you do get a warning. The next one is through your skull."

"That one even made me jump." Lilith stepped away, towards Leo, and took a place behind the dangerous weapon. "Let's play a game. Who wants to live? Amuse me."

"Huh?" Axel shook his head, trying to get the thought of his head being splattered out of his mind. "What's that supposed to mean?"

"I want to live," Terrence muttered. "What do I need to do?"

"Amuse me," Lilith reminded him. "Use Omer. Tap into your animalistic instincts."

"She'll kill us no matter what we do. Don't you see that?" Axel was defeated. "Why would we do her bidding? We'll end up just like the kid on the table here."

"That's the negative attitude that will get you dead. Do I get a weapon?" Terrence held both of his empty hands in the air. "You want me to use these?"

"If you appreciate your life, you will. Hurt him. Amuse me. Try to win your life back," Lilith taunted. "Like I said, this is for my entertainment."

Terrence closed his fists, cracking open a fresh scab on his wrist. Omer was lying down, and he was standing, so the angle was all off, but his hand collided with the side of the boy's chin, knocking his head sideways. The way he was strapped down didn't allow Omer's body any movement, but his neck made up for that, as his ear collided with his shoulder.

"Boring," Lilith looked displeased. "I want to see blood."

"Break his nose or something, Axel. Make her happy. We have teeth. We have fingernails. Those can be weapons, right?" Terrence was still shaking his own pain away from the impact of his fingers crashing against the hard bone. "Bite him! Claw him! Do something!"

"No! I refuse! Why? What's the point?"

"That is the point. There's no point other than her breaking us, molding us into what she wants us to be." Terrence's words grew heavy. "Watch this," he said as he stuck his fingers in Omer's mouth.

The boy must have been heavily sedated, because he didn't respond.

"Is he dead?" Axel asked. "No, wait, I hear him breathing."

Terrence grabbed onto one of Omer's front teeth. "This is harder than it looks. Have you ever tried to pull a tooth that wasn't loose?" His fingers kept slipping off due to saliva buildup, but tried and tried again, wiggling the tooth the best he could, trying to free it from the gum line.

There was an audible crack, accompanied by a guttural sound that escaped Omer's mouth.

"I did it! Look!" Terrence held up his prize tooth for all of them to see. "Are you entertained now?"

"Better," Lilith noted. "Not quite there, though."

"What's wrong with you?" Axel sounded angry. "You're hurting this kid for no good reason."

"There it is, Mr. Axe. The response I don't like. The response I did not want. Do I need to remind you that your life is at stake?" Lilith asked from a distance. "Are you a man?"

Axel raised his hand, and flipped her the bird, his middle finger blatantly pointed towards her.

"Boss, let me blow it off, please?" Leo sounded like a child anxious to open a present. "I can do it from here. *Pew, pew.*" The way the bodyguard used a high-pitch tone to sound like a fake gun, made his comment comical.

"Is that so? You're so untouchable way over there on that side of the room. You're brave from so far away."

Axel's snide comment made Lilith gasp.

Before anyone had a chance to react, Axel wrapped his fingers around Terrence's neck, and began to strangle him. "This is all your fault!" Axel screamed. "Screw you!"

Their bodies fell to the floor, Axel, younger and more athletic, on top of the lawyer, squeezing, so the man couldn't suck oxygen into his lungs. Terrence raised his fists to fight back, but he was clearly at a disadvantage.

In her usual calm manner, Lilith waved a hand over the two fighting men. "Okay, put a stop to this. It's gone far enough."

Axel felt Leo's strong arms lifting him off the older man. "Get off my dad! You'll pay for this!"

Axel took a blow to the back of his head, knocking him unconscious, but not before his mind was swimming with the idea of Terrence being Leo's father.

Actualities

Cold, Bitter, Truths

"You're right, Lil," Terrence stood on the other side of the window of the punishment room, looking in on a naked Axel. "It is more fun when they're here of their own volition. It takes everything to the next level. It's almost like they hate themselves, which is better torture than I could ever come up with. And the look on his face. At first, he thought he was selling me out, then he thought we were victims together. Priceless, the look on his face when he realized I betrayed him. What a mind game. A rollercoaster of emotions for him. Me too. Haven't had this much fun in a while."

"I told you so," she replied nonchalantly. "I wish you had picked a stronger subject, though. I did lose the bet fair and square. You fully warned him about me, yet he agreed to come here. For money. What an idiot."

"And you," Terrence shoved his finger in Leo's face. "You did a great job with the makeup. I really did look like you had beat me up. But did you have to knock the wind out of me when I was in the wheelchair?"

"Sorry, old man. It was all for show," Leo shrugged. "It was still worth it though, right? Those last few moments before I knocked him out. When he finally realized how badly he messed up. I think we fried his brain circuits, him trying to make sense of it all."

"Yeah, yeah. I suppose. Do I get to push the button?"

Terrence gladly pressed the button, the one that activated the punishment. Cold air was pumped into the room. Music was so loud that it would make Axel feel like his eardrums were bleeding. The strobing light rotation of darkness and blindness would drive him mad.

"Oh, he's awake,' Lilith observed. "Let's get Omer. He's still very much alive. That one is a fighter. We'll make Mr. Axe watch, make him fearful of his own fate."

"I'll go get him. You want some power tools, too, boss?" Leo asked.

Lilith nodded.

"I'm so proud of my boy, Lil," Terrence said, pulling her in for a hug. "You've really shaped him into a man. This is a perfect vacation. I couldn't have asked for anything better."

"Like father, like son. It was my pleasure. Why deprive ourselves of human nature? If we were animals in the wild, we'd do the same to breed. To eat. Who says humans can't have fun?"

More of Omer's Suffering

It was impossible to tell whether Axel was watching through the window. The room was soundproofed, but the vibrations were felt in the next room. There was light in their room on the other side of the glass, but even they found the small amount of light flashing annoying.

Terrence tried his best to look inside the window, but his eyes didn't adjust before looking away. "I assume he's watching. What else does Axel have to do in there? I would think this would be fun to watch."

Leo never minded a bit of hard work, and Lilith had been very specific with her request. She wanted a wooden plank to be propped against the wall. The bodyguard/ assistant didn't ask why.

"Stand him up," she told Leo. "I want Omer standing against the wood. Hands over his head."

There was simply no fight left in the boy. Maybe it was a blessing that she had given him something to ease his pain. It had been for her own selfish reasons, to shush his cries, but still a benefit to the employee that was being given his exit package.

She used a nail gun, and placed it directly in the center of the boy's palm, his fingers curled outward. Five inches of cold metal plunged through his hand, attaching him to the wood. Whatever pain killer he had in his system was starting to wear off because he cried out and curled his fingers.

A fingernail even snagged on the head of the nail.

Terrence wanted to participate, so he had the privilege of using the nail gun on the other palm, also above Omer's head. Streaks of blood ran down the boy's arms, collecting in the hair of his armpit.

"Omer, can you hear me?" Lilith screamed in his face. "If you can pull your hands free, I'll allow you to walk out of here, right now. A free person."

Omer acknowledged her words with a moan. His eyes scrunched up and he yelled in agony, but he did try pulling his hands away from the wall. All that he managed to do was rip the holes of his palms wider. Thicker, blacker blood dripped down his arms.

"Look at his cock! Or should I call him an eunuch? No, he still has half of it. So he's not fully castrated. That looks painful," Terrence said. "The way you spit it out, when you bit off, on the glass was a great effect."

"He's watching!" Leo exclaimed, pointing at the window. "Check that out. Axel is standing up by the window. Give him a show!"

"I like the idea of them having each other to watch. One while nailed to the wall, the other in the punishment room. I think I have plans for Axe. Do what you wish with Omer, just don't kill him," Lilith left the room, leaving father and son alone with the victim.

"What do ya think, old man? What do you want to do with him?"

"I want to kill him, but she said no. It's been forever since I killed someone," Terrence replied, picking up a hammer and a chisel. "I think I'll do some more on that dental project I started."

Leo watched as his father placed the chisel between Omer's lips. The boy closed his mouth, but Terrence didn't care. Whether it damaged his mouth or lips wasn't of his concern. As long as the boy bled.

The hammer *pinged* as it hit the head of the chisel, driving the metal wedge into Omer's face hole. His mouth was reddened, almost as bad as Lilith's as when she bit off his cock. Sloppy tears mingled in the blood, pink dripping off the boy's chin.

This time, Terrence handed Leo the chisel, and his son placed it square with Omer's hip bone.

"Hurry son! Axel is still watching!"

The hammer *pinged* again, this time the large flat side breaking skin, and possibly bone beneath it.

Omer lost his footing where his leg gave way, pulling his body weight down on the nails.

"He's too skinny, anyway," Leo commented. "Fragile bones and all. Think I could dig some of that hip bone out? Hand me a knife. I want to see what he looks like on the inside."

Father watched as his son flayed the broken skin, plunging the blade into the iliac crest (upper area of hip bone) and brought it down in vertically and downward slices. He took his time, not going too deep, and making horizontal slices of flesh, then pulled them back slowly with his hands.

The flesh peeled away like old wallpaper glued to a wall. Slow and methodically was the best option.

"Dad, check out these tight stringy things! You suppose they're ligaments? Tendons? I know the soft squishy parts are muscle."

"I love seeing you so happy, son." Terrence bent down to view the inner hip with his own eyes. "I'll be danged! You did crack a bone! Look at that! Give that one another smash! It won't kill him!"

Leo placed the tip of the chisel into the bone fragment, swinging the hammer harder this time.

An audible crunch made Omer cry out in pain. "Just kill me! Please!"

"Didn't you hear her, boy?" Terrence asked. "She wants you alive, and she always gets what she wants."

Then Terrence started a conversation with his son like they weren't in the process of making another human suffer. "Hey, you know, I have a full week off from work. I'd like to play some golf, or at the very least hit a few balls around."

"Sounds fun. I'm in. I wonder what the boss has in mind for Axel? By the way, he's cowered in a corner now, not watching us."

"Hmm, I don't know, but I'm sure it will be a treat. Why don't we go and find out?"

"Sure, let me wash my hands first. I'll be down there in a minute."

Terrence mocked his son. "Wash your hands? Why? I enjoy the feel of dried-up blood coating me like a second layer of skin. Smells nice, too."

"Yeah, yeah, and at least I can relax now. I get some time off work, too. It's just us on the island, so I don't have any security to be doing."

As they exited, they left the light on in Omer's room, so Axel could see the damage they were capable of, and what possibly could be in store for him. That was Lilith's idea. Her motto was that psychological torture could be even worse than physical pain.

Axel's Suffering

"A pet? I think that's a lovely idea!" Terrence exclaimed, taking a sip of his Scotch. "Can you work out the details, Leo? To make your job easier?"

"Yeah, I have some ideas."

++++++

Making Axel a Pet

"I've taken pity on you, Axe," Leo said as he injected his arm with a syringe and pushed down the plunger, releasing a clear liquid. "You'll still be awake, but you'll feel good. Well, better than feeling every moment of this."

Axel's eyes fluttered into the back of his head as he felt the effects of the drug. He was semi-awake, but whatever he was given made his body feel euphoric.

"You just lie still. I have to make some modifications for this to work. First, I'm cutting your Achilles tendons. To basically make it impossible for you to walk. It was either that or cut off both your feet."

"Huh? No." Axel's words came out tired and slow.

Leo used a handheld pair of pruning shears and positioned both sides of the blades around the backside of Axel's ankle. The moment he closed the grip, bringing the two blades together, skin split and blood flowed. "Was that deep enough? I have to admit, I've never done this before. I'll snip again, further into the tendons and muscles, just to make sure I've done it properly."

The second incision was deeper, releasing darker blood. "Now, I'll take the blowtorch to it. Just to stifle the bleeding. Boss wants you to live for a long time. Can't have you bleeding out on me."

The flame hissed to life, boiling blood and blackening Axel's flesh. "It'll probably be tender for a while. The blisters, maybe third degree burns. But you'll live. Okay, now the next foot…"

Leo got to work, making both feet equally unusable. "You're not screaming too bad. The drugs are working. That's great. Next problem is your hands. If I cut those off, you might bleed to death, and it would be impossible for you to crawl around. I'll just snip off all ten fingers."

The fingers were thinner than the backside of his ankles, so Leo assumed they would cut off easier with the pruning shears. He was wrong. Bones and joints got in the way, but he managed to remove all the fingers and both thumbs at the joint nearest the palm.

It wasn't straight across snips that worked. He had to make multiple slices, then angle the blades to follow the curvatures of the knuckle joint. It took time and patience, but Leo was proud of his finished product.

He had done what he set out to accomplish. Two hands that could no longer make a fist, grab/hold objects, making it less likely the new pet could do much to attack his new owners.

By the time he cauterized all the wounds, the smell was stuck in his nose. Burning human flesh. A mixture of rotten egg and copper aroma. Leo enjoyed it.

Axie-Poo, The Pet

Axel laid on his belly like a snake. Even if he wanted, he couldn't stand on his feet. His hands were still sore, open wounds where each finger used to be, leaving a trail of blood in their wake from crawling.

"He's perfect, Leo!" Lilith was excited. She patted her new toy on the top of his head, rustling his dirty and matted hair. "Your new name is Axie-Poo. Got it? I even got you a new leash," she said as placed something thick around his neck. "It's equipped with the ability to shock you. Let's test that out."

Lilith pressed a button, and Axel's body vibrated in rhythm with the voltage surging through him. "That works. I'll still want you nearby, Leo, just in case, but when I don't need him, I'll lock him in his room. If you're a good boy, Axie-Poo, I won't turn on the punishments in your room. But if you're a bad boy, it will be cold, loud, and hell on your vision. Got it?"

Still reeling from the shock, Axel could barely respond. "Huh?"

"He'll be good, I'm sure of it," Leo added. "If not, I'll chip every bone in his body. He could live a long time like that, same as Omer upstairs. He's watched me do it. It's not a pleasant sight."

"Terrence, lover, piss in his water bowl. Put some of the kibble in the other bowl."

"You will eat whatever I give you. And drink whatever I give you. I know you'll need water at times. Dehydration can be a pain, and I want this experience to last. For now, though, crawl over to your bowls like a good boy."

"Huh?"

Lilith raised a leg and stomped Axel on his butt. "Do you want me to shock you again? Crawl over to your bowls!"

Axel raised his ruined hands, and applied pressure to his elbows to slither the floor like a snake. His feet hung behind him like masses of useless body parts. The crawling was slow, but he made it to his bowls, and the acrid smell of Terrence's urine infiltrated his nostrils. The cauterization of his absent fingers had cracked, leaking bodily fluids.

"Drink! Or I'll shock you!"

Axel learned that drinking from a bowl was no easy task. Not only did he have to raise his neck, he had to stick his tongue out far enough to reach the liquid, to lap up the piss.

"I'm sure when it's water, you'll learn to make your tongue scoop up the liquid, like an improvised bowl or something. Once you learn that skill, I'm sure I'll make good use of your tongue."

Terrence and Leo were laughing so hard that Axel could barely hear Lilith's words.

"What do we think? Who wants to play with our brand new Axie-Poo?"

"Me. I have some ideas," Terrence said between his guttural belly laughs.

Golfing with Axie-Poo

"Fore!" Terrence swung his 1-wood driver. "Oh, my slice is way off," he criticized himself, laughing.

Axel was on his back, a tee with a white ball had been placed in his mouth, held in place with straps so he couldn't move his neck or open his mouth.

The golf club had missed the ball completely, the aim too low, the wooden head of the club smacking Axel in the side of his jaw, pulverizing bone, breaking the joint of his jaw. A dark welt formed instantly, taking up his entire cheek.

"Yeah, that's got to hurt," Terrence said with no sympathy. "Leo, get out here! He's too fragile. This won't work."

His nearby son stepped outside the patio door. "What's wrong? I already told you, just hit the balls over the pool. Who cares if they go in the ocean? They'll either float back to the beach, or not."

"No, it's not that. I'm breaking Axie-Poo's face, and I doubt Lil will like that."

"Oh yeah, I see, ouch. What's he chewing on? Pieces of broken teeth?"

"Probably. Do me a favor. Flip him over. My back isn't as young as yours. And I'm nowhere near as strong."

Leo flipped Axel, and placed the tee between his butt cheeks, trying to get it positioned to a ninety-degree angle. The sharp side of the tee must have punctured something, but it made him bleed.

Once the ball was balanced, Terrence swung again, this time his low swing smacked Axel's butt cheeks, smacking them together so brutally that they made clapping sounds. The smacked cheek reddened, leaving behind a nasty bruise.

"Yeah, that's much better. Thanks, son. You want to take a swing?"

Bath Time w/ Axie-Poo

"You sure are a stinky pet!" Lilith screamed loudly while holding her nose for effect. "We need to give you a bath!"

Leo held the pet's leash that was wrapped too tightly around Axel's neck, but Lilith held the remote that would send electric shocks through the man's body via the shock collar.

"Drag him on in here," Lilith demanded as she led them into the downstairs bathroom. "We really need to get this done. It's stinking up the whole house."

The acrid aroma of urine, provided by Terrence and Leo, painted the white bathtub a very brilliant yellow. It wasn't half-full of piss, but it would be enough for Axie-Poo to climb into and get wet.

"Don't help him, Leo. Make him get in by himself."

Crawling on all fours had been Axel's new way of life, painful still with his burnt finger nubs and ruptured Achilles tendons.

"Get on in, dog, or I'll shock you," Leo threatened.

Axel had to raise his hands onto the lip of the bathtub and apply pressure to his palms, which resulted in his wounds reopening and spilling red in the urine, giving it an orange tinge.

Leo laughed the entire time and watched while Axel positioned himself sideways, and tried to raise his knee to the top of the tub like a dog using the bathroom on a fire hydrant. One hand and one knee were now on the porcelain, but Axel wasn't strong enough to push through the pain and lift himself inside.

Lilith pressed the button and sent voltage through her new pet's body, which sent him sprawling backwards, falling on his back, causing his hands and feet to flail in the air, wildly.

After the shock ended, Axel found strength to speak, exhausted and lying flat. "If you shock me near liquid, I could die!"

"I knew we should have cut out his tongue," Lilith remarked to her bodyguard. "Maybe another time. Anyway, I'm not sure if the shock collar will electrocute you in water. Plus, it's not water. It's piss. So many variables. Would it kill you? I'm not an electrician, so I can't be too sure. Help him get in there, Leo."

The security guard didn't have to be told twice, so he lifted the pet under his arms and threw him into the urine with a splash. Axel's face hit the liquid first, and it burned his eyes and ran upwards his nostrils.

"Should I hit the button, Leo? Will it kill him?"

"Probably. And I thought we still had that other thing planned. That playtime thing for later."

"Yeah, you're correct," Lilith agreed. "I wish your father was still here to see this. Drain the tub. Wash him properly with water and soap. He does stink."

"Sure thing, boss." Leo got to work, but not before holding Axel's head under the foul substance. "I will, but let's have some fun with him first. You want to start setting up the playground? Or do you want me to do it?"

"I'll do it," Lilith replied. "I am looking forward to this."

Playtime w/ Axie-Poo

"Do you think five hundred of them are enough?" Leo asked, amazed at what he was seeing.

Axel was still leashed and collared on all fours, his eyes as large as half-dollars.

The majority of the floor was covered with mouse traps, all set to spring when touched. "I can't crawl across that! Can I at least get some clothing?"

"Yeah, eventually we'll remove his tongue. But this is a good thing, Axie-Poo. If you do this, I'll feed you a proper meal tonight. And you won't have to sleep in the punishment room." Lilith spoke calmly, but her words were sharp with her own delight.

"Okay, dog," Leo patted the pet's wet hair. "Start crawling. You have to make it to the kitchen for your meal."

"And if I refuse?" Axel was scared and found bravery in his fear.

"Then I chip away at every bone in your body. Same as I've been doing to Omer upstairs. I know you know, because you've been watching me do it. Get to it. We don't have all night."

Axel wanted to use logic and tread carefully on the traps, but they were so close together that it would be impossible to not get stung by the traps. The only thing he could think of was to reach his arms as far as he could, and try to use the least amount of crawls as possible.

Axie-Poo extended a hand, his palm coming into contact with a mousetrap. It *snapped* into place, the metal bar closing onto the wooden plank, pinching his skin in the process. It stuck in place, creating an angry red wound. "Nope! I'm not doing it! Kill me now!"

"Kill you now? No. She spent a long time setting this up. You're doing this." Leo pulled on the dog leash, but Axel refused to move.

Leo got upset, and lifted Axel by his hair, pulling the scalp from his cranium. Axel's neck craned upward, and his body fell limp. That didn't deter the strong bodyguard from lifting the man's body from the ground and throwing him into the pit of mousetraps.

There were so many snapping sounds that they clinked like dominoes, a chain reaction of sounds. Axel screamed and groaned, but could barely be heard through the laughter. Once the dust settled, Axel remained still, afraid to move and being pinched further.

The pet held his head above the carnage for as long as he could, but between the pain of his nude body being nipped and bitten by metal springs of pain, his face fell downward. *SNAP! SNAP! SNAP!*

His nose was the first to catch a mousetrap, but then his chin also triggered a trap.

"I want to see the damage," Lilith said impatiently. "He's lying down and I can't see anything. Stand him up or something, Leo. Let us see."

Leo tugged on the leash, tugging sideways, flipping the pet on his side, and then jerked up, landing Axel on his back.

"Look at his dick!" Leo taunted. "Look at that! The head is swollen, trapped in there. Like a little mousy!"

The penis and testicles were both covered with the small wooden bases of the traps, but where they were caught between the metal and wood, they swelled in size and color (purple). Blood leaked from cracked skin, specifically the head of his penis.

The scrotum was bunched up, multiple mouse traps, four, stuck on snagged flesh pulled taut giving a clear outline of both interior testes.

"His toes too!" Lilith pointed out. "I can barely see his chest. I bet he has over fifty mousetraps covering his body. Probably more now, since you flipped him on his back. I say we leave him there for a bit. Let's see how long he lies there until he starts crawling again."

"Yeah, I probably don't even need to hold the leash anymore. I bet he stays there for a while. You want to place bets? I bet he doesn't move until morning."

"I'll take that bet, Leo, but I bet he moves before that."

Leo raised his eyebrow and looked at his boss. She pushed the button and activated the shock collar, making Axel's body convulse, this time triggering more mousetraps.

"I win, Leo. What do I get?"

Axel remained on his back, staring at the ceiling, feeling pain radiate through his body, and listening to his captors. "Please, just kill me." His words were weak and they didn't hear him.

Future Plans (During Another Show)

"Look at him in there. He's trying to take the mousetraps off, but it's nearly impossible without fingers. His body is covered with them. I'll stay true to my word, though," Lilith remarked, staring through the glass window into the punishment room. "I won't turn on the lights, music, or the ice cold air."

Axel placed both of his palms around the mousetrap, squeezing the head of his penis. He tugged and pulled and yanked, but all it did was run the metal clasp down the shaft of his manhood. His penis elongated, rubbery and limp, now black in color from lack of blood flow.

"I think he wants to die. So I'll go to work on Omer here and remind the pet what's in store for him when we tire of him." Leo sliced a square of flesh away on Omer's lower rib cage, and scraped away muscle until a couple of bones were visible. "Hand me that chisel, would you? Think I should hammer directly into the bones, or between them?"

"Not between them. That could puncture a lung. Why kill him this soon?"

"Good thinking boss. When is dad's next vacation? Are y'all planning something fun?"

"Of course we are, dear. Of course, we are."

"Crap! He's bleeding pretty bad. Get me that blowtorch, or would you like to do the honors?"

Lilith turned the flame on, marring pink flesh until it blackened beneath the heat. "Look, it's good and ashy here. Why don't you chisel into that? Make me a big cloud of black crumbs." She enjoyed the familiar smell of cooking human meat.

A note from my dark mind

We all learned that Terrence was Leo's father. It was one hilarious GOTCHA! Moment (in my opinion), like when you jump out behind something to jump scare someone. But Terrence played the long game, getting inside Axel's head, winning the bet with Lil he could get the PI to her island, despite how dangerous (he did warn him). Axel thought he would get rich by offering her the lawyer, but he thought wrong.

Here's my question, though. Was Lilith Leo's mother? It was alluded to that she and Terrence were past lovers/ current lovers. Does that make her Leo's mother? I left that one open. I sometimes like to allow the reader's imagination to do some of the work. Some of y'all that I've chatted with online/ emailed, etc… have greater imaginations than I do. Very impressive. Anyhow, some would say she was not his mother because the sex scene. Who would write an incest sex scene between mother/son? Or was Lil just his father's lover?

Who knows? Not even me.

Based on Lilith's perspectives, I'm going with her being his mother. But maybe she wasn't.

And I'm basing that on the fact that when asked why she does what she does, she had no good reason. ('Entertainment' I think she said). Does everything have to have a reason? Some readers would say yes. Some would say no. Why do I read books? Why do I play video games? Why do I watch movies? Entertainment.

Can people kill purely out of boredom?

I get it that Lil was rich and had a safety net on her own private island, but could you imagine being that rich? How would you entertain yourself if you had all the money in the world? It would stand to reason that those people tire of the things that entertain us (the ones in a normal tax bracket). For example, some people love to travel. If you did it everyday on your own private jet, would it eventually bore you? The common person doesn't travel but maybe, what, twice yearly for a vacation? If even that often.

Now, most people wouldn't kill to entertain themselves. But I think Lil makes for a fun character, one that I like to dislike. Maybe we'll see more of her in the future? Maybe that's a bad idea. Who's to say?

I try to put out at least one novella a month, so be sure to keep up with me for new releases.

If you want to keep up with my releases, I'm on various forms of social media, etc…

If you're like me and don't spend much time on social media, here's a good old fashioned email. sharoncheatham81@gmail.com.

I read often and love Goodreads, too. If you want to keep up with what I'm reading, I'm Sea Caummisar on Goodreads.

Until then, Stay Dark My Friends,
See ya next read,
Your Friend,

Sea Caummisar
Contact Info for Sea Caummisar
Facebook (Sea Caummisar)
Twitter (@seacaummisar)

See ya next read

Printed in Great Britain
by Amazon